Beginning School

written by Irene Smalls • illustrated by Toni Goffe

Silver Press

Parsippany, New Jersey

*For Miss Loretta Abbott, Kindergarten Teacher, P.S. 90,
Harlem, New York circa 1955 who helped teach me,
"I love you Black Child."*

I.S.

Text © 1997 by Irene Smalls

Illustrations © 1997 by Toni Goffe

Published by Silver Press

A Division of Simon & Schuster

299 Jefferson Road, Parsippany, N J 07054

Designed by BIG BLUE DOT

Manufactured in the United States of America

ISBN 0-382-39328-7 (LSB)   10 9 8 7 6 5 4 3 2 1
ISBN 0-382-39330-9 (JHC)   10 9 8 7 6 5 4 3 2 1
ISBN 0-382-39329-5 (PBK)   10 9 8 7 6 5 4 3 2 1

Library of Congress Cataloging-in-Publication Data

Smalls-Hector, Irene.

Beginning school/by Irene Smalls; illustrated by Toni Goffe   p. cm.

Summary: When Alicia makes a new friend and becomes involved in the fun activities
of an integrated kindergarten, she soon forgets her former anxieties about beginning
school. [1. Kindergarten—Fiction. 2. Schools—Fiction. 3. Afro-Americans—Fiction.]

I. Goffe, Toni, ill. II. Title

PZ7.S63915Bg   1996   95-25762   [E] dc20   CIP   AC

a   n

b   o

Dear Reader and Friend,

Welcome to Beginning School!

    Come with me and you shall see
What the first day of school will be.

    There will be books and boys,
girls and toys, and special things to do.

    You'll find giggles and games, trips
and names, and magical musical stories.

    You'll make new friends and
laugh and learn with hugs and holidays.

    So come and play.
You'll want to stay all day.

    It's time to begin school.

Sincerely,
Irene Smalls

THE FIRST DAY

Alicia and her mother got up early. They didn't want to be late. Today was Alicia's first day at school. "Mommy, when I'm at school what will you do?" "I will bake a cake and think of you," Alicia's mother answered.

"But Mommy, what will I do in school?" "You will make new friends and learn many, many things," her mother said, smiling.

Alicia wasn't so sure she would have any fun in school. But her mother had told her she was a big girl now. Alicia knew that being big meant going to school.

Alicia and her mother walked to school. Alicia's mommy took her to her class's line.

n
o
p
q
r
s
t
u
v
w
x
y
z

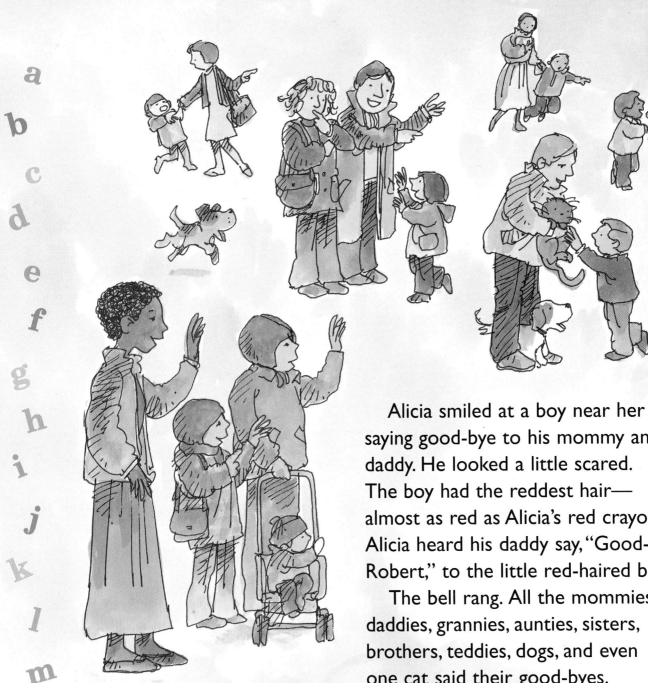

a
b
c
d
e
f
g
h
i
j
k
l
m

Alicia smiled at a boy near her saying good-bye to his mommy and daddy. He looked a little scared. The boy had the reddest hair— almost as red as Alicia's red crayon. Alicia heard his daddy say, "Good-bye Robert," to the little red-haired boy.

The bell rang. All the mommies, daddies, grannies, aunties, sisters, brothers, teddies, dogs, and even one cat said their good-byes.

n
o
p
q
r
s
t
u
v
w
x
y
z

"Welcome to school, girls and boys! I'm your teacher, Miss Abbott. This is my helper, Mrs. Jones." And in came Alicia, Dante, Debra, Luisa, Henry, Sara, Susan, Eric, Robert, Nyeilla, Jamal, José, Malcolm, Martin, Maria, and all the kindergarteners.

"Good morning, Miss Abbott. Good morning, Mrs. Jones," the children all said.

a
b
c
d
e
f
g
h
i
j
k
l
m

Alicia looked around the room. There was so much to see. There were alphabet letters, numbers, paints, a piano, books, animals, and cubbies to put their things in, too.

Miss Abbott said, "Each of you has your own special cubby." She showed each child a cubby just for them. Alicia liked having a place that was just for Alicia. Everything was just her size, too. Robert made a face when Miss Abbott showed him his cubby.

"Someone seems to have lost his smile," Miss Abbott said looking at Robert's face.

"Oh, oh. Can I…?" Dante cried,
wiggling.

"Oh, yes," Miss Abbott said, "If you have
to go to the bathroom, please just raise
your hand to ask.

Next, Miss Abbott showed the children
around the room. She showed them the
Story Rug, the Library, the Playhouse, the
Computer, the Painting Place, and the
Science table with a real snake.

"And this box is the Lost and
Found where things lost are found
again," the teacher said, smiling.

n
o
p
q
r
s
t
u
v
w
x
y
z

"Please take your seats," Miss Abbott
said. "It's time for morning snack."
Miss Abbott and Mrs. Jones set out
the snacks.

After snack time the children sat on the Story Rug.
Miss Abbott read them a story called "Jonathan and His
Mommy" about a little boy taking a walk in the city. "I will
read you a story every day," Miss Abbott told them.

Next, the children were taught a song by Mrs. Jones about making friends. Alicia, sitting next to Robert, asked shyly, "Will you be my friend?" Robert nodded yes. Alicia liked to make new friends.

n o p q r s t u v w x y z

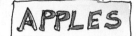

MILK

APPLES

a
b
c
d
e
f
g
h
i
j
k
l
m

After singing the children went to eat
lunch in the cafeteria. Miss Abbott
showed them exactly where to sit.
A helper opened Malcolm's milk carton.
Another helper gave Alicia a knife, a fork,
a spoon, and a napkin.

Alicia ate her lunch happily seated
between Robert and Luisa. Robert
showed them his new tooth.

After lunch was play period in the gym.

When they were back in class, they listened quietly as Miss Abbott played some soft music and read them a funny poem that made Alicia laugh.

n o p q r s t u v w x y z

a
b
c
d
e
f
g
h
i
j
k
l
m

Later, the children learned about the different shapes by coloring rectangles, circles and triangles.

When they were finished, Miss Abbott said, "Please clean up now." The children put away their papers in their cubbies.

"You all did a wonderful job! Thank you," Miss Abbott said.

The bell rang again, "Time to go home," the teacher said. See you tomorrow."

"Good-bye Miss Abbott. Good-bye Mrs. Jones," the children all said as they left the classroom.

Alicia ran back and gave Miss Abbott a hug. Alicia liked Miss Abbott, and Alicia liked school.

When Alicia went outside, her mother was right there, waiting for her.

n
o
p
q
r
s
t
u
v
w
x
y
z

a
b
c
d
e
f
g
h
i
j
k
l
m

THE SECOND DAY

Alicia left her mommy and ran to meet her teacher.
Robert was there too. Only he still wasn't so happy.
Alicia held out her hand. Together Alicia and Robert
walked to class.

That morning the teacher gave each
student a large piece of paper to write
on. Alicia made a huge A. "Aaaalicia," she
said. Miss Abbott put a blue sticker on
Alicia's paper. Alicia giggled.

n
o
p
q
r
s
t
u
v
w
x
y
z

After Reading was Music. Letter sounds, music sounds, Alicia loved to hear the pretty songs Mrs. Jones played on the piano.

a
b
c
d
e
f
g
h
i
j
k
l
m

"Recess," Miss Abbott called. The children jumped rope, played catch, and ran races.

Alicia fell in the school yard and scraped her knee. Alicia started to cry. Mrs. Jones took her to the School Nurse, who washed it and put on an orange bandaid.

n
o
p
q
r
s
t
u
v
w
x
y
z

After lunch, Alicia played a game on the computer
with Luisa.

Next, the children gathered for Show and Tell. Alicia
and Luisa both raised their hands. Miss Abbott said,
"We will take turns." She called on Luisa. Then she
called on Alicia.

a
b
c
d
e
f
g
h
i
j
k
l
m

In the afternoon they had Assembly. Some older
students danced. Everybody clapped.

After Assembly was Science. The class watched as their pet snake shed its skin. Alicia felt the old skin. It was rough and bumpy. Robert was afraid to touch the snake's skin. Miss Abbott said, "That's all right, Robert. You don't have to touch it if you don't want to."

n
o
p
q
r
s
t
u
v
w
x
y
z

THE THIRD DAY

Robert began to like school too. When the teacher
came in, Robert was sitting in the Lost and Found box.
"Robert, what are you doing?" the teacher asked
laughing. "I found my smile, Miss Abbott," Robert said,
wearing the biggest grin.

That morning the class went on a field trip to Fairmount Park.

Later Alicia and Luisa
played on the seesaw.

The entire class had a picnic in the park.

a
b
c
d
e
f
g
h
i
j
k
l
m

n
o
p
q
r
s
t
u
v
w
x
y
z

After the picnic, back at school, there was a surprise.
Alicia's mother came to class. It was Alicia's birthday.
Everyone sang "Happy Birthday" to Alicia.

Alicia's class took a big yellow school bus straight down Broad Street to the Please Touch Museum. Robert's daddy and Alicia's mother came along to help.

a
b
c
d
e
f
g
h
i
j
k
l
m

Alicia, and her friends, Robert, and Luisa walked together through a giant wheel.

THE SECOND MONTH

The children had their pictures taken. Alicia felt like she had always been in Miss Abbott's class.

n
o
p
q
r
s
t
u
v
w
x
y
z

There was a Halloween party in class too. Everyone wore costumes. Robert was a bear, Alicia was a princess, and Luisa was a clown.

HOLIDAY TIME

Two weeks before vacation, the class started making holiday decorations. They made stars, masks, and colored menorahs.

The last week of school, Miss Abbott's class celebrated five times. First was Christmas.

Next was African-American Kwanzaa.

Then Hanukkah.

Then the Festival of the Three Kings from Puerto Rico
(Dia de los Trés Reyes)

and after that Chinese New Year.

n
o
p
q
r
s
t
u
v
w
x
y
z

School was over for the holiday vacation. It was time to go home. Alicia loved the holidays. But Alicia was glad that after vacation she was going back to school.